Enid Blyton

The Disappearing Hats

illustrated by
Chris Rothero

AWARD PUBLICATIONS LIMITED

Once upon a time, in the Village of Get-About, there was a hat-shop. Two gnomes owned it, Sniffle and Snuffle. They made excellent top-hats in all colours – blue, pink, yellow, and green, for the folk of Get-About went to a great many meetings and parties, and wore top-hats very often.

And then a strange thing happened. The top-hats belonging to the people of Get-About began to disappear in a very peculiar way!

THE DISAPPEARING HATS

Burly-One, the gnome, had just bought a magnificent green one with a yellow band round it. He wore it to a meeting in the next village and felt very smart indeed. He came home and hung it up as usual in the hall. The next day it wasn't there!

Then another hat disappeared. This time it was Curly-Top's hat. He was a pixie and had a very choice top-hat – pink with a blue band, and he had stuck a little feather in at the side. He had put his in a box on a shelf in his bedroom – but bless us all, when he looked in the box the next day, the hat was gone! The only thing in the box was the little feather.

THE DISAPPEARING HATS

When Curly-Top and Burly-One met and began to tell one another about their vanished hats, two others came up and said theirs had gone too!

'I put mine on the kitchen table,' said Bong, the brownie. 'And this morning it wasn't there.'

'And I put mine on the knob at the end of my bed,' said Chortle, the elf. 'And I know it was there when I went to sleep, because my wife said to me, "Chortle,

you've put your hat on the knob again instead of in its box." So I know it was there – and this morning it was gone!'

'And there's the party today at Lord High-and-Mighty's,' groaned Burly-One. 'What are we to do? We *must* go in top-hats!'

'We'd better go to Sniffle and Snuffle and see if they have any hats to fit us,' said Curly-Top. 'I don't expect they will have.'

They went to the gnomes' shop and explained to them about their vanished hats. Sniffle and Snuffle listened and looked very surprised indeed.

'Now the thing is, Sniffle and Snuffle,' said Bong, 'we've got this party this afternoon. Can you possibly let us have top-hats in time?'

'I suppose you'd like them just the same as your others?' said Sniffle.

'Yes,' said everyone.

'Well, we'll try to manage them in time,' said Sniffle. 'But we are afraid we will have to charge you more than usual, as we shall have to work so hard.'

'Oh dear!' groaned Chortle. 'Well, I suppose it can't be helped.'

THE DISAPPEARING HATS

Exactly ten minutes before Curly-Top, Burly-One, Chortle, and Bong were ready to set off to their party, their hats arrived from Sniffle and Snuffle. They each put them on in delight. Really, they might have been the same hats as those they had lost! They fitted perfectly.

THE DISAPPEARING HATS

Now that night three other hats disappeared belonging to Fee, Fi and Fo, three goblin brothers. They were terribly upset because they had to go to a most important meeting that day – and how could they be seen out without their fine top-hats?

'I put mine in my bedroom on the top of the wardrobe,' said Fee.

'And I hung mine on the chair,' said Fi.

'I don't know where I put mine, but it was *some*where!' groaned Fo.

'We'd better go to Sniffle and Snuffle and see if they can let us have hats in time,' said Fee.

So off they went – and the two gnomes
promised to work hard and send three
hats in good time.

'But we shall have to charge you more
money,' said Sniffle.

THE DISAPPEARING HATS

Now as more and more top-hats
disappeared the people of Get-About
Village became very angry. They lay in
wait for the robbers whom they thought
must come to steal their hats – but never a
robber did they see! It was all most
peculiar.

The only people who didn't mind about the disappearing hats were Sniffle and Snuffle, who did a roaring trade, and charged every one more than usual because they were so busy and had to work so hard.

THE DISAPPEARING HATS

At last Fee, Fi and Fo, whose hats had disappeared for the second time, went to visit the wise woman, Dame Thinkitout.

She listened to their tale and then nodded her head. 'So you want to find the thieves?' she said. 'Well, tie a long, long string to your hats, goblins, and then, when they disappear, follow the string and you'll find the thieves at the end of it!'

'What a good idea!' said Fee, Fi and Fo.

They went home and each of them carefully tied a very, very long string to his hat. One end was round the hat, and the other was tied tightly to the bed knob.

Nothing happened that night – but the next night the goblins were awakened by a strange whistling sound. They lit a candle. Their hats were gone!

'Quick!' said Fee, tumbling out of bed. 'We must follow the strings!'

They found that the strings went out of the window – down the garden, across the road, over the long meadow, down the hill – and into – where do you think?

THE DISAPPEARING HATS

Why, into Sniffle and Snuffle's shop! Yes, really!

THE DISAPPEARING HATS

The goblins peeped into the shop through a crack in the curtain. They saw Sniffle and Snuffle there. Sniffle was standing in the middle of the room, chanting a magic rhyme, and Snuffle was standing with his arms out to catch the hats that came in at the window!

'Oh! the wicked robbers!' said Fee, Fi and Fo angrily. 'They make our top-hats – and put a disappearing spell in them so that they can get them back – and then sell them to us again for more money than before!'

THE DISAPPEARING HATS

The goblins all climbed in at the window and began to shout at the surprised gnomes.

'Robbers! Thieves! Wait till the people of Get-About hear what we've found out! Yes – just wait till tomorrow morning!'

THE DISAPPEARING HATS

'Mercy, mercy!' begged the two gnomes, pale with fright.

'Certainly not!' said Fee, and pinched Sniffle's long nose. He had wanted to do that for a long time. 'Give us our hats!'

The goblins took their hats, put them on, and stalked out of the shop. 'Aha! You wait till tomorrow!' said Fo.

You can guess how angry the folk of Get-About were when they heard all that Fee, Fi and Fo had to tell them.

They marched to the gnomes' shop next morning – but it was closed! A notice hung outside. GONE AWAY. YOU CAN ALL EAT YOUR HATS!

'What a cheek!' snorted Chortle, in a rage.

'Well, we can at any rate use the hats they've had to leave behind!' said Bong.

THE DISAPPEARING HATS

There were heaps of top-hats in the shop. The folk of Get-About tried them on. There were enough for everyone to have two or three.

THE DISAPPEARING HATS

'I'm glad I pulled Sniffle's long nose last night,' said Fee. 'I wish I had pulled Snuffle's too!'

Nobody knows what became of the two bad gnomes – and a very good thing too!

For further information on Enid Blyton please contact www.blyton.com

ISBN 0-86163-710-0

Text copyright The Enid Blyton Company
Illustrations copyright © 1998 Award Publications Limited

Enid Blyton's signature is a trademark of The Enid Blyton Company

First published in *Enid Blyton's Happy Story Book*

This edition first published 1998 by Award Publications Limited,
27 Longford Street, London NW1 3DZ

Printed in India